# Cattle Farms

Cheryl Jakab

NELSON
CENGAGE Learning
Australia • Brazil • Japan • Korea • Mexico • Singapore • Spain • United Kingdom • United States

**Cattle Farms**

Text: Cheryl Jakab
Editors: Emma Short and Rochelle Ransom
Design: Jess Kelly
Series design: James Lowe
Photo researcher: Corrina Tauschke
Production controller: Lisa Porter
Reprint: Siew Han Ong

**Acknowledgements**
The author and publisher would like to acknowledge permission to reproduce material from the following sources:
AAP Image/AP Photo/Silvia Izquierdo: p. 13 (bottom); AAP Image/Lyn Durham: p. 11 (inset left); Corbis: pp. 1, 9 (main), 9 (top right), 10, 11 (bottom), cover; Fairfaxphotos/ Sandy Scheltema: p. 12; Fairfaxphotos/SMH/Jon Reid: p. 11 (top); Getty Images: pp. 5 (top left), 13 (top); Photolibrary: pp. 3, 4–5 (main), 4 (inset left), 4 (inset centre), 4 (inset right), 5 (centre left), 5 (bottom left), 5 (centre right), 5 (bottom right), 6 (main), 6 (top right), 6 (bottom right), 7 (top), 7 (bottom), 8 (top), 8 (bottom), 14–15 (main), 14 (bottom left), 14 (bottom right), back cover.

Every effort has been made to trace and acknowledge copyright. However, if any infringement has occurred, the publishers tender their apologies and invite the copyright holders to contact them.

**Fast Forward Independent Texts Level 8**



For product information and technology assistance,
**in Australia call 1300 790 853;**
**in New Zealand call 0508 635 766**

For permission to use material from this text or product, please email **aust.permissions@cengage.com**

ISBN 978 0 17 017946 1
ISBN 978 0 17 017896 9 (set)

**Cengage Learning Australia**
Level 7, 80 Dorcas Street
South Melbourne, Victoria Australia 3205

**Cengage Learning New Zealand**
Unit 4B Rosedale Office Park
331 Rosedale Road, Albany, North Shore NZ 0632

For learning solutions, visit **cengage.com.au**

Printed in Australia by Ligare Pty Ltd
2 3 4 5 6 7 22 21 20 19

## Contents

Chapter 1 **Cattle Farms** .......... 4

Chapter 2 **Cattle Herds** .......... 10

Chapter 3 **Cattle Farms and the Environment** .......... 12

Glossary and Index .......... 16

CHAPTER 1

# Cattle Farms

Some of the food people eat comes from cattle farms. There are cattle farms in countries all around the world.

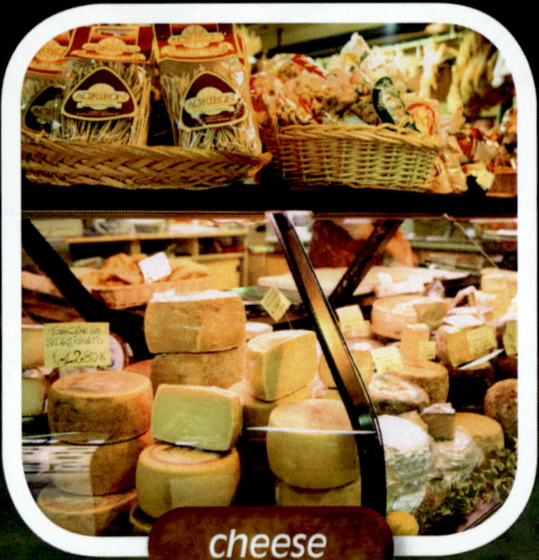

*cheese*

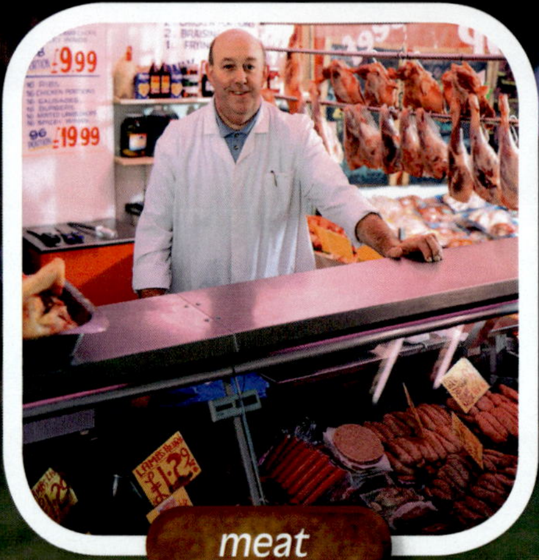

*meat*

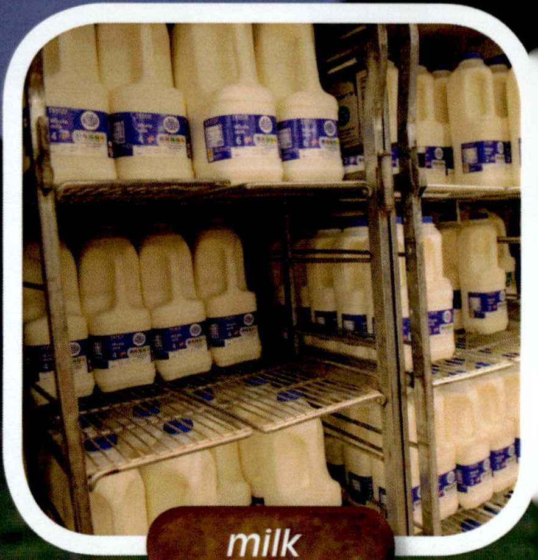

*milk*

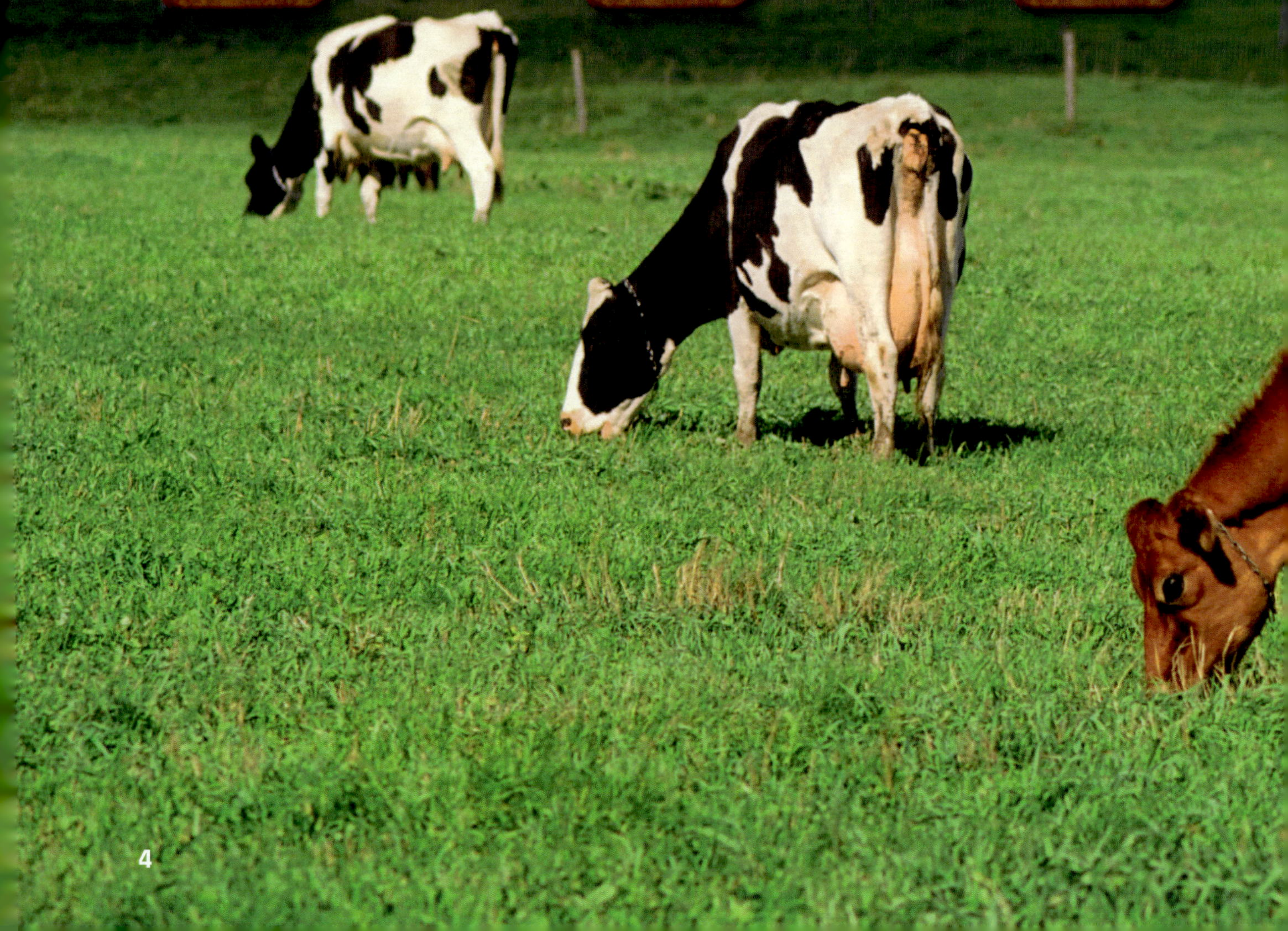

Cattle farms are different all around the world. The cattle and the **farmers** are different, too!

Masai tribesman in Kenya

cattle farmer in Australia

cowboy on a ranch in the USA

cattle farmer in England

cattle farm in Switzerland

Meat and milk come from cattle. Many people like to eat these foods.

The meat from cattle is called beef.

Butter, cream and cheese are made from milk.

Some cattle are not used for food.

leather bag, gloves and belt

leather jackets

Cattle must be well fed.
Some cattle eat grass all day.
Some cattle eat **hay** or **grain**.
On small farms,
farmers feed cattle by hand.
On big farms,
farmers use machines
to feed cattle.

Farmers must milk their **dairy cattle**
every day.
They can do this by hand.
But today,
many farmers use machines
to milk their cattle.

CHAPTER 2

# Cattle Herds

Cattle live and feed
in a group called a **herd**.
A herd of cattle can be big or small.
Farmers move the herd
around the farm
to find good grass
for the cattle to eat.

On small farms,
farmers can work with dogs and horses
to move the herd.
On big farms,
farmers can use machines
to move the herd.

*Some farmers round up cattle with motorbikes.*

*Some farmers use helicopters to round up cattle!*

# Cattle Farms and the Environment

Some people believe
that cattle are bad
for the **environment**.
The cattle dig up the ground
with their **hooves**.
This is bad for the plants
that are food
for other animals.

*Farmers let their cattle eat the grass in this **national park** for many years.*

In some countries,
trees are cut down
to make space
for more cattle farms.
This can be bad
for the environment, too.

Trees may be burnt to clear land.

There have been cattle farms
for many, many years
all around the world.
We need cattle farms
for food such as milk
and meat.

But cattle farmers
need to take care
of the environment, too.

## Glossary

| | |
|---|---|
| **dairy cattle** | the kind of cattle that give us milk |
| **environment** | the natural world around us |
| **farmers** | people who work on farms |
| **grain** | seeds from plants like wheat, corn, oats or barley |
| **hay** | dried grass |
| **hooves** | the feet of cows, horses, donkeys or pigs |
| **national park** | an area that is protected for wildlife and the environment |

## Index


dairy cattle 9
environment 12–13, 15

farmers 5, 8–11, 15

grain 8
grass 8, 10

hay 8
herd 10–11

machines 8–9, 11
meat 6, 14
milk 6, 9, 14

plants 12